We Called
Him Bunny

Richard Andersen

Levellers Press

AMHERST, MASSACHUSETTS

Published by *Levellers Press*, Amherst, Massachusetts

Cover painting by Dix McComus
Cover design by Steve Strimer

Printed in the United States of America

ISBN 978-1-937146-50-4

This one is for us.

I

BUNNY

I was born to run. Fast. That's why people call me Bunny. I've been running for as long as I can remember. To and from school, on errands for Ma and Pa, even around the block while waiting for my friends to come out and play. One time I ran all the way to John  Brown's historic house and back home again just for the fun of it. You name it; I ran it.

Sports were my specialty. It didn't matter what shape the ball. As long as I was holding it when the game was on the line that was all my teammates cared about. They knew I was their best chance of winning. Always. And being given all those balls as often as I was, I could soon throw them almost as well as I could run with them. Would you believe in my first year of high school I played on the varsity football, basketball, and baseball teams? No one in the history of Springfield

Tech had ever done that. Nowhere else in Springfield either. And I didn't just play; I was a star.

Once, during the final minutes of a football game, the coach sent in a play he made up on the sidelines. It was called, "Give the ball to Bunny and block." They did and I did and three games later we were the city champions. In all those games, no one ever tackled me from behind. No one. That's when everybody—friends, teachers, coaches, even newspaper reporters—started calling me Bunny.

Everybody except Ma. She was one of the few people who called me by my real name. Of course, like most moms, she thought I should spend less time running and throwing and more time reading and writing. She thought sports were a waste of time because people of color couldn't make much of a living from them. "Ernest," she used to say, "a bunny ain't nothin' but a rabbit. You ain't no rabbit. Why you let people call you that? Can't you aim no higher? Twenty years from now, people will think Satchel Paige is some kinda handbag. Now Booker T. Washington? That's a name people will not soon forget."

Pa called me "Bunny" but not when Ma was around. "You is big and strong 'cause your ancestors was bred to work long and hard as slaves in the South. That was long time ago. Before the Civil War. Which you don't know nothin' about 'cause you too young."

I'll tell you something I do know about: those ancestors must've been fast on their feet. You had to run to escape on the Underground Railroad. Ma said our ancestors were smart too. They settled in Springfield because they heard John Brown lived here. They believed he would protect them from being sent back to the plantation. They didn't know John Brown had already left the city to fight against the spread of slavery in Kansas. I didn't know until I read about it in junior high school that he'd been hanged in Virginia. That's where our ancestors' plantation was.

I made my name in football but mostly everybody remembers me from baseball. Getting under fly balls, cutting off line drives, and retrieving grounders was as easy for me as turning on a radio. And a lot more fun. My speed also helped me be a better hitter. Sure outs for others were base hits for me. Sometimes I'd be able to force an infielder to rush the ball and make a bad throw to first. That made my teammates cheer louder than if I'd gotten a hit. They liked seeing the look of frustration and disappointment on the player's face, and they reminded him of his error every time he came up to bat. Not me. I never said a word. I imagined how I'd feel if I made a bad throw. I'd feel sorry for the guy. But I never said anything because that's the way the game is played, and once on base, you have to think how you're going to steal second. No pitcher ever picked me off, and no catcher ever threw me out. Not even on a pitch out.

For Pa, baseball was my ticket to success. "Readin' and writin' is good," he told me more times than I can remember, "but they don't help you get no job. You get good enough to play in the Industrial League, that be your salvation. Boss look after you then. Don't give you no hard work. Make sure you be well rested. Play better for the company. Not wind up like your pa, chaufferin' white folks around 'cause factory work done wore you out. Not have to allow your wife to wash white people's dirty clothes 'cause you can't make enough dough to pay the bank and put food on the table by yourself."

I was confident I could do both: read and write well enough to please Ma and play baseball well enough to get a cushy job in a factory that had a team in the Industrial League. That would make Pa happy too. And I wouldn't have to do work that rich white people are too lazy to do for themselves. I never thought I'd say something like that—I grew up with white people—but that's what a place like Gastonia can do to you. Once it gets inside you, you can't get it out. Not ever.

II
JOHNNY

I never liked Bunny Taliaferro. Not really. How can you like someone with a name like Bunny? He wasn't even Italian. And I don't care if he was only fifteen or sixteen at the time. He looked like he was going on thirty. If you told me he was married and had two kids, I would've believed that before I believed some of the stories people told about him. You'd think there had to be two Taliaferros. Practically every time you opened to the sports pages of the *Springfield Daily News* it was Bunny did this or Bunny did that. Bunny 21; Central 7 ran one headline. And no last name neither. Just Bunny. If you listened to the journalists, you'd think he was the next Jim Thorpe.

I knew Bunny when he lived next door and didn't have enough sense to go by his middle name. We even walked to school together, but that was only until a desk opened up for me at Our Lady of Hope. I had to repeat a grade and walk two miles to get there, but getting out of the public and into the Catholic school was worth every step. All I learned there was new. I read my first story without needing pictures to explain the words, and before the year was out, I was doing fractions and decimals while Bunny was still adding and subtracting. Of course we got whacked a lot with rulers, pointers, and other boards of education, but that was the price you paid to make sure you got into Cathedral. Only hell was worse than being banished to one of Springfield's public high schools. That's how we were made to feel back then. Tech and Central and Commerce were where kids like Bunny had to go as punishment for being Protestant. They couldn't get into Cathedral, and they couldn't get into heaven either. At least not in the places closest to God and the angels and the saints. If I knew then what was to become of us, I would have said that Bunny's winding up at Fisk Tire and my representing Springfield in the state legislature was as much a proof of God's favoring Catholics as Gene Tunney twice beating Jack Dempsey and Knute Rockne coaching Notre Dame to victories over any infidels that got between the Fighting Irish and their goal line. I don't think that way anymore. Not after what happened in Gastonia.

Yeah, Bunny could certainly run. He hardly did anything else. But straight-out speed wasn't all he had. He could dash and dart too. And at few times better than when Mr. Taliaferro chased him around their backyard. We lived next door. I would watch the action from my desk on the top floor of our double-decker. It wasn't pretty, and it almost always ended the same way. First, there'd be an angry shout from a room inside Bunny's house. A threat invariably followed: "When I get my hands on you ..." The screen door would then slam, and by the time I looked up, Bunny would be standing hind the big oak that shaded his entire yard.

Next came Mr. Taliaferro. His belt in one hand and his loosened pants in the other, he'd fly off the back porch as if he'd been shot out of a cannon. I'd think Bunny wouldn't live to run another errand, but he'd zig and zag around the yard with Mr. Taliaferro lunging and flaying in hot pursuit. Only for Bunny it seemed more like a game. He never fled the yard, and sometimes I swear he even slowed down enough to make his father think he could catch him. The old man couldn't catch his breath let alone Bunny.

After several minutes of hopeless effort, the winded Taliaferro would stop, put his belt back in his pants, and order Bunny to stand in front of him. For reasons I could never understand, Bunny did exactly what he was told. What followed was worse than the belt or any punishment ever administered at Our Lady of Hope. Bunny would use his arms to protect his body and his hands to protect his face while his father wailed at him as if he were a punching bag. He never cried; he never fought back; he never said a word. He just stood there and took what he knew was coming. If the thrashing got too bad or went on for more than a few minutes, Mrs. Taliaferro would come out and pull her husband away from the boy.

Bunny could run, Bunny could feint, and, yes, Bunny could take a hit. Not many people knew that back then. Or for some time to come. Before Jackie Robinson broke the color barrier with the Brooklyn Dodgers in 1947, there was a lot of talk about why African-Americans would never make it as professional athletes. Some claimed the blacks didn't have the mental toughness to compete above a certain level. Even if they were physically able, they couldn't withstand major league pressure. That they were never given a chance to be tested in that deep down way that doesn't so much build character as eliminate those who don't have it rarely entered the debate. Others said the coloreds couldn't take the pain, that they'd fall down the moment a tackler touched them rather than try to gain a few extra yards by running over him; that they'd jump out of the batter's box rather than get hit by the ball that would send them to first base; and that they'd let someone else vie for a rebound rather than find their noses in the way of a flying elbow.

Of course there were exceptions like Jack Johnson. He'd get in the ring with anybody. But Johnson never got hit. He'd dance around every great white dope until his opponent was exhausted. Then he'd pummel the poor guy with punches until he collapsed on the canvas. That was no way to box. Even when Bunny led the Springfield Tech football team to city championships in 1934 and 1935, there were doubters. People said if he wasn't so scared of being hit, he wouldn't have been able to run as fast as he did. Others credited the big guys he had on the line opening holes for him. The fact that no one could catch Bunny once he was in an open field was used to confirm these views.

III
JOHNNY

Bunny and I were still in knickers when our mailman saw him throw a snowball to scare away a squirrel from the birdfeeder in the Taliaferros' backyard.

"Did you see that?" the mailman asked Mr. Taliaferro, who was standing on the back porch.

He hadn't.

"Do it again," the mailman told Bunny.

Bunny packed another snowball, wound up, and hurled it through the air. It struck the birdfeeder so hard, seeds splattered on the ground.

"Again," said the mailman.

Again Bunny made life easy for junkos.

"Your boy's got some arm," the mailman exclaimed.

Mr. Taliaferro grunted in agreement and went into the house as if to say hitting a birdfeeder with a snowball was no big deal, but he might've also been annoyed with the mailman for noticing something about Bunny that he hadn't. It was hard to tell what Mr. Taliaferro was thinking at times. Or why he sometimes behaved the way he did.

Bunny was the same way. He threw snowballs at that birdfeeder all winter, moving farther and farther away as his speed and accuracy increased. By the time spring rolled around, he'd switched to a sock filled with mud and was throwing from the dirt street that ran between our houses.

"This used to be mine," the mailman told Bunny.

It was a baseball glove. Bunny's first. And the first one I'd seen with only three fingers. Everyone else's had four.

"Your mom is going to have to re-stuff the palm with rags, but you won't need 'em much if you learn how to use the web properly."

Inside the glove was a ball. The first Bunny ever owned.

"Cover it with tape, and the stitches will hold longer," the mailman advised. "And replace that birdfeeder; it looks like it's been through the Second Battle of the Marne. Get yourself a tire or an inner tube."

Bunny got an old tire from Kelleher's Garage and strung it up on the tree so the hole would be the same distance from the ground as a strike zone. The big old oak was his backstop. Hitting the hole with an object he could grip firmly and didn't change its shape as it flew through the air was a lot easier than nailing a birdfeeder with snow or mud. The baseball also required less of an arc to reach its target. It wasn't long before Bunny was throwing ropes as straight as any clothesline from the same distance as the pitcher's mound is from home plate. And it wasn't long after that when he almost never hit the rim unless he wanted to.

"You keep firing like that," the mailman told him, "you're going to have to get a license for your arm."

Bunny got something better: his dad. Perhaps because of the mailman's initial interest, Mr. Taliaferro showed a deeper interest in his son's interests. "You got the Taliaferro arms," he told his son after the mailman left. "The Taliaferros was the biggest and strongest of the slaves 'cause they did the hardest and heaviest work. They be the blacksmiths. That's what Taliaferro means: blacksmith. They was given that name because that be their job on the Virginia plantation. They overseer, he was Italian. He give it to them. But now they be givin' their arms to you all these years later. Blacksmith arms for throwin' hardball strikes."

Baseball didn't stop the beatings—not completely—but it did put enough time between them for Bunny and his dad to get to know and understand if not always appreciate each other better. Bunny came to accept his father's wanting the best for him even if sometimes he didn't have the best way of showing it—he wasn't the only kid whose dad beat him—and Mr. Taliaferro realized his son had some special talents that he could use to make something of himself and bring honor to the family name. Now, when he wasn't running where other people walked, playing whatever sport was in season, or throwing his baseball through that tire, Bunny was pitching to Mr. Taliaferro. Of course no pitch was ever thrown quite as hard as the old man had been able to hurl it when he was Bunny's age, and Mr. Taliaferro had no second thoughts about showing his son how to scratch a ball on his belt buckle, apply spit to it without the umpire catching him, or even brush back batters from the plate, but Bunny felt his dad's quest for him to win at all costs was a small price to pay for not having to retrieve every ball he threw. Bunny never even had to leave the mound he'd built on top of what one day would be part of a stone curb. And once his father cut down a three-foot swath from the hedge running around the Taliaferros' yard, the boy no longer had to throw over it. Nothing stood between him and pitching success now. "There's a place waitin' for you in the Industrial League," Mr. Taliaferro would tell his son for the umpteenth time. "They say Bosch goin' to need a pitcher in a couple of years now that Brady's best days is behind him. That happen to us all. It happen to me an it goin' to happen to you. But you is goin' to have a longer meantime 'cause you got the arm of a Taliaferro."

Bunny heard his dad, and he was grateful for what he might have inherited from his ancestors, but it was his mom's words about aiming higher that he took to heart. His sights were on that baseball diamond in his future where every pitch he threw was a strike, every swing he took was a home run, and only the ball was white.

IV
DANNY

Imagine. It's 1932. You're fourteen years old. There are no Ipads, no Iphones, no Ianything. No one you know has a telephone or a radio. Television is only an idea. Soccer mom isn't even that. If you want to go anywhere, you either walk or hitch a ride on the rear platform of a trolley. Your food is kept in a steel box that has to be filled with ice, and your heat comes from a furnace that has to be stuffed with coal. The ice and the coal are delivered by trucks when the gas needed to run them is available. Your home has plumbing, but your family keeps an outhouse in the backyard just in case the electricity or water is shut off.

You live in a section of Springfield known as Hungry Hill, and it's no picnic. Especially during the Great Depression. A lot of people are out of work and money is hard to come by. Food is so scarce your mom has to stand in a breadline every day for hours while your dad tries to find what work he can in better neighborhoods: washing windows, mowing lawns, cleaning cars, even walking dogs.

But there's one lack you don't have: people. Everybody pitches in to help whomever they can whenever they can—even to the point of leaving hand-me-down clothes and food that has to be eaten that day inside your screen door without you knowing who put it there. You're mom's sister housed your come over parents when they arrived from Ireland, and they weren't in a place of their own for more than a few weeks when one of the seven sons of your mom's oldest brother showed up direct from County Kerry. He stayed for two years and would have stayed longer if he hadn't found a job in Ohio—the first place he'd been where he didn't see a "No Irish Need Apply" sign. The next day, three Keyeses left for Cleveland.

You've been playing baseball with Bunny and Johnny for as long as you can remember. They're both pitchers. Good ones too. So good that when teams are chosen in Van Horn Park, Bunny and Johnny are always the first to be put on opposite sides. Then Johnny's team gets the next two choices because Bunny is three times as good a hitter, runner, and fielder as any single player. Bunny throws harder than Johnny and is tougher to hit, but Johnny has more than one pitch so you never know which one he's going to throw. Better placement too. He tries to fool you rather than overpower you. He's also more competitive than Bunny. Anytime his team loses, he takes it personally. Make an error, and he won't talk to you for the rest of the game. Sometimes longer. Bunny's teams, of course, don't lose. Not often anyway.

If you want to beat a team with him on it, you've got to keep the ball out of his hands and away from his bat.

You and Tony King are on your way to Howes Sand when you run into Bunny and Johnny. They're heading to Van Horn for the first pick-up game of the day. You try to convince them to go with you. Tony's heard from Franny Luce about a new excavation pit where huge amounts of dirt are being dug up by machines with big shovels and transported along cables to bins where it's dumped into trucks. One of the cables runs about twenty feet above a hill of soft sand. Even though you've never been to Howes Sand, you say, "We can all ride the cable out over the hill and then jump in the sand."

Johnny isn't interested: "I gotta work on my pitches."

Neither is Bunny: "I gotta league game; I wanna get in some batting practice."

You tell Johnny, "You can work on your pitches this afternoon," and you tell Bunny, "Your game isn't 'til tonight."

"You go if you want to go so bad," Johnny says as if he can't wait for you to leave. "Yeah," says Bunny, "If we win tonight, we get to compete for the trip to Yankee Stadium. You think I'm gonna pass up Babe Ruth and Lou Gehrig to play in some sand?"

He has you there, but you don't think about that because something has crumbled inside you. The red heat of embarrassment has risen on your face. You feel like Johnny and Bunny think you're not as good as they are because you want to do something other than play baseball for a change. They got the whole summer to play baseball. You wonder where the buddies are who stole potatoes with you from Grower's Outlet, baked them in the fires you'd built at Bare-Assed Beach, and ate them like apples beside the Connecticut River. What happened to the pals who, like you and Tony, couldn't afford sneakers but didn't let that stop them from taking on all-comers in their stocking feet on the basketball court at the downtown Boy's Club?

You should have thought less and listened more. At least to the part about playing at Van Horn instead of Howes Sand. When the cable from which you were hanging suddenly changed direction and ran your left hand through one of the pulleys, you lost four fingers. It also took the top off from the middle finger of your right hand. And you never did get to jump in that sand. You remember what Tony said when you got out of the hospital two weeks later? "You ain't never goin' to play in the big leagues now."

V
BUNNY

Did you ever like someone, but you couldn't tell the person because you were afraid they wouldn't take you seriously, and it was better to like them without their knowing it than to know they might not like you in return? That's how it was with me and Sweets. Though she didn't know until years later, I'd been calling her by that name since the very first time I saw her. Coffee with cream on the outside, she had to be filled with sugar on the inside. I just knew it. Especially when she smiled, which she did when I asked if I could carry her books. She handed them over, and I walked her all the way to her locker inside Commerce High, but what could I do next? I was only twelve!

Sweets doesn't remember that day, but it floated my boat for years. I imagined us holding hands in Van Horn Park, watching a ballgame at Yankee Stadium, even being married and making feet for shoes. Whenever we passed on the street, I'd say hello and tip my cap if I was wearing one, but still being a kid I never had the courage to walk with her again. I didn't even know her name. When I found out, I preferred Sweets. She did too. Bunny and Sweets. It sounded better than Ernest and Julia. It's also says more about who we are.

My time for high school came in the fall of 1934. Football season. Tech had a good team but had never won a championship. That's where I came in. Although I was pretty sure I would make the team by the end of our first practice, I wasn't a starter until after coach called my name during a game that was already well in hand. He wanted to take a look at what some of his subs could do while the other team still had their first string on the field. I was given the ball twelve times, and two of those times I crossed Central's goal line. Coach was pleased, but he took me out of the game because he didn't want to be accused of running up the score. "You never want to win too big," he told me apologetically. "It makes people look forward to getting back at you the next time you play them."

We won our first five contests with the toughest game being against Agawam, a team that hadn't scored a touchdown in two years. Talk about pressure! We didn't want to go down in history as the school they finally beat. Or even scored on. Coach told us, "These guys are losers, and you've got to remind them they're losers. Let the possibility of winning enter their heads, and it's going to be a long afternoon."

We did, and it was. No one caught me from behind, but I never got a chance to break into the open field either. Not for the whole first half. I'd never been hit so hard or so often. Sometimes by several people all at once. There were times I didn't see daylight unless I was flat on my back. How could these guys have lost so many games?

Mistakes. That's what did them in. We scored twice toward the end of the second quarter on an interception return and a fumble recovery. You would've thought a completely different team wearing the same uniforms showed up for the second half. Our offense took over, and I spent most of the last quarter warming the bench so others would have a chance to play. Final score: Tech 33; Agawam 0.

By Columbus Day weekend, we were the highest scoring team in the state and playing the only team that hadn't given up a single point all year: Commerce. It was also their Homecoming Game. So many people wanted to see it that extra bleachers had to be installed along the sidelines and behind the end zones. I'd never seen a thousand people in one place, but there was only one person I was on the lookout for. Would she be there? Would I play well enough for her to notice me? How would she recognize me in a uniform with my helmet on? What if she saw me as someone who was trying to prevent Commerce from making the city playoffs? What if she didn't give a fig about football and was home reading a book?

Not a chance, and by halftime I found out why: Sweets was the Commerce High School Homecoming Queen. Sitting in an open car being driven around the perimeter of the field, she was the one person in the whole stadium everyone cheered. More beautiful than ever, she passed right in front of our bench as we waited to start the second half. I took off my helmet and tried to tip it the way I would have my baseball cap had we met on the street, but it fell to the ground and I had to grapple around my teammates' legs to get to it. Fortunately, she didn't see any of this. Her eyes were on the handsome escort waiting for her with a bouquet of roses at the fifty yard line. Could that be her boyfriend? Why hadn't I gone to Commerce instead of Tech? Why couldn't I have been my parents' sixth child instead of their eighth?

We were only down 7 to 0. There were still thirty minutes to shine. If I could score a touchdown, I'd dedicate it to Queen Sweets like a knight who'd just unseated his opponent in a tournament. She couldn't help but notice me then.

I scored three. After the first touchdown, I ran before her throne in the stands, put my helmet under my arm, and bowed from the waist. Some of the people on the Commerce side booed me because they thought I was being a show off. Coach didn't know what I was up to. "You trying to let their fans back in the game?" he asked as I returned to the Tech sideline.

After second score, I removed my helmet, bent my knee as I bowed toward my lady, and swept my hand six times along the goal line as if to say, "Every point is for you." Perhaps because the game was now out of reach, there were fewer boos from the Commerce side and even a few cheers.

The third touchdown inspired me to kneel before Queen Sweets on one knee and raise my helmet in a salute. Now there was nothing but applause. The crowd finally got it: this boy is in love. Sweets got it too, and a red rose landed at my feet. Today it's pressed into a copy of *Don Quixote* that has this sentence underlined on the page; "Only those who attempt the absurd are ever capable of achieving the impossible."

VI
JOHNNY

Bunny's girlfriend was a beauty. And four years older. A senior while he was just a freshman. How did he do it? I understand she was at the City Championship game in which he scored the go-ahead touchdown and went to all his home basketball games as well. He told Tony his shooting percentage was higher in every game she attended. Some guys have all the luck.

I was too light for football and too short for basketball, but Danny said if we could make names for ourselves on a baseball team, we could get girlfriends too. Perhaps not homecoming queens, but maybe princesses who'd come to our games and root for us like Bunny's girlfriend did for him. Danny said if we could play well enough to letter, we could get one of those school sweaters so the girls would know how lucky they were to have us as boyfriends. We'd be good ones too. We'd let them wear our sweaters to every game they attended.

My chances for a letterman's sweater were better than Danny's because, next to Bunny, I was probably the best pitcher in Springfield. One of them anyway.

Danny used to be a solid hitter, but when he lost the fingers on his left hand, he couldn't control the bat as well. He could still field though, catching slower hit balls with his bare hand and depending on the popsicle sticks he stuffed into the fingers of his glove to snare line drives and high-hopping grounders. Playing for Classical would also give him more time on the field. They had such lousy teams, few students tried out for them.

Cathedral's weren't much better and in a much tougher league. I knew I had to be at my best if I was going to letter. Just making the team wouldn't be enough. Soon there were tires hanging from two trees in the neighborhood with Bunny's going up and down according to the season: chest high for football, closer to the knees for basketball, and back up to the waist for baseball.

During the football season, Mr. Taliaferro would brace himself against one side of Bunny's tire so his son could work on his blocking from the other. "You gotta do mo than just run if you wants to be best," he told him. "The mo you can do, the mo ways you got to help the team. Good blocks is what makes good plays." Bunny used the tire during the basketball season to practice his bounce passes, and Mr. Taliaferro also used it to teach him how to pass behind his back. "The mo tools you has the mo ways you gets to use 'em," he explained. "Them other teams won't know what to do if they don't know what you goin' to do."

Those words came through my window from the Taliaferros' backyard, but they might as well have descended from heaven. Even though the old man had been talking about football and basketball, what he said often pertained to baseball as well. I wrote down his words and stuck them to my bulletin board for inspiration: "The more you can do, the more ways you've got to help your team." So simple, so obvious, and yet so crucial for success: "Other teams won't know what to do if they don't know what you're going to do." Mr. Taliaferro was a genius.

So while Bunny's tire moved up and down according to the season, mine stayed in the strike zone. Every day I threw at its center. I knew I could never hurl a baseball as fast as Bunny—nobody could—but I could improve on my curveball and learn a few other pitches besides. If the batters didn't know when my fastball was coming, it didn't have to come in as hard. By the spring, I'd developed a slider and a forkball, could make do with a halfway decent change up, and even toss an occasional knuckleball though I never used it in an organized game. Too risky. Send one in that doesn't float, and the batter is looking at a ball with home run written all over it.

"Winners don't quit and quitters don't win."
"Nobody remembers who comes in second."

Technique wasn't enough; you had to have attitude to win. Mr. Taliaferro knew that. Every night, after saying my prayers, I'd read all the things I'd heard him tell Bunny. They were like prayers to myself to help me be the best player I could be. I might not have had as much talent as Bunny or Tony or some of the other guys, but I could develop more heart. That was just as important as skill. Maybe even more important.

"Show me a good loser, and I'll show you a loser."
"Pitching is the art of instilling fear."

Yes, there had to be a certain amount of meanness in your heart if you lacked talent and wanted to compete with the best. You couldn't think twice about doing whatever it took to win. Even if that meant purposely throwing at a batter to back him away from the plate or teaching him a lesson about what happens to pitchers who throw at anyone on your team. To be a winner, you have to hate losing. You have to hate the happy expressions on the faces of those who beat you more than you enjoy the thrill of victory. You have to refuse to lose. That says it all. I wrote those words—Refuse to Lose—on the thumb of my glove so I could remind myself anytime during a game where my head should be. Did I say game? Baseball was a war, and I was going to be Cathedral's biggest weapon.

VII
DANNY

You're lucky and you know it. You lettered your first year at Classical, but you never would've been asked to play for the American Legion team if Post 21 hadn't wanted a player from each high school in Springfield and you were the only one on the varsity young enough to meet the age requirement. You don't let that bother you. What's important is what you do the next time you're on the field, not what you didn't do the last. When your time comes, the difference of a few fingers isn't going to stop you from competing with the best. You'll make sure of that. You've already replaced the popsicle sticks in your glove with wooden rulers that, with a bit of file work on both ends, reach from the tips of your fingers to the palm of your hand. No more line drives blowing through your mitt now. You wonder why you didn't think of it sooner.

It could be worse. You imagine what it's like to be Johnny. He wouldn't be a starter if Vic Raschi was a year older and the schedule wasn't so packed with double headers Bunny wouldn't have a chance to rest between outings. And what if Bunny had an off day? Or got injured? It hasn't happened—he won every game he started at Tech, was never relieved, and set league records in every hitting category—but you never know.

The Legion teams are all from different towns and made up of all-stars he's never played against. One of them could finally get to him. Still, you'd think Coach Babe Steere was doing Johnny a favor by asking him to play when Bunny didn't. No matter. He'll get his chance. He'll show them all. Even if Cathedral hadn't done so well during the school season, Johnny was still the best pitcher in the Catholic League.

Post 21 lost in the State Championship game in '33, but with Bunny and Johnny on the team, it could go all the way. Bunny, Johnny, and Tony King. Tony was last year's leadoff hitter and this year's Captain. You couldn't ask for a better second baseman or a better friend. Remember how he behaved when you lost your fingers at Howe Sands? Anybody else would've run for help. Or fainted. Not Tony. Remember how he took the shirt off his back and wrapped it around your hand to stop the bleeding? He then picked up the severed tip of the middle finger on your right hand, pressed it onto its stub, and told you to hold it there as best you could until he got you to the hospital.

It wasn't easy. When the Liberty Street driver wouldn't let you on his trolley because he didn't want to have to clean up any blood you might spill, Tony pushed you right past him and into a seat.

"This trolley ain't goin' nowhere as long as you two are on it," the driver threatened.

"Then this kid is goin' to bleed to death and you're goin' to be responsible," Tony replied.

That was all it took.

When you got to the hospital, your legs were a little wobbly, but Tony was there to help you into the emergency room. No one had ever seen anything like it. Not so much your hand but your fingers. Tony had put them in his pocket before leaving the excavation pit. Now they were staring at you from the top of the admitting desk. You'd never seen them from such a distance. Glistening with sweat, covered with sand, and laced with blood, they looked as if they might belong to someone else. Perhaps this is why you didn't feel any sense of loss. At least not until you saw the severed top of the finger on your right hand looking at you from the opposite side of where it was supposed to be. That's when the floor came at you faster than any pitch you ever saw.

VIII
BUNNY

Pa was thrilled. Undefeated in my first year of varsit-play and selected to start for the American Legion team that would represent Springfield, my name would be in the *Springfield Daily News* all summer long. Employers with teams in the Industrial League would be reading about me and thinking about how they could recruit me. "You don't need no high school diploma to work in a factory," Pa pointed out. "Maybe one of the owners offer you a job before you graduate. You be getting paid to play. That make baseball count where it count most: in the bank. Maybe there be a bidding war. Maybe I make some money too. See which company pay me the most to make you sign wit them."

Ma was furious. All this talk about making money was taking my eyes off the prize. Baseball wasn't the reason I was going to school, and I wasn't going to school to work in a factory. "What happens you get hurt?" she asked. "You think any factory's goin' keep you on if you can't play? What good baseball do you then?"

Ma had a point. But so did dad. And I didn't know what I wanted to do with my life other than play baseball often and for as long as I could. I sometimes talked to Sweets about someday playing in the Negro leagues, but how did I know if I would ever be good enough? I was only fifteen.

That's how the future Mrs. Taliaferro got the idea of writing to Rube Foster. He'd founded the Negro National League in 1920. His answer was a short one: "No professional player I know ever came out of an industrial league." That was all I had to hear. That and the slogan which was written under the league's logo at the top of the page: "We are the Ship; all else the Sea." I wasn't sure exactly what it meant, but I got the feeling that the future was in my hands. As captain of my own ship, I could set sail in whatever direction I wanted. I decided to go in two at the same time: stay in school until I graduated and continue playing baseball with the hope of making more money in one of the Negro leagues than I could ever make in a factory. When I got too old to play professional ball, I could pitch in the Industrial League. The bids would be even higher then.

That pleased Pa. Sort of. I think he had his eye on some of the money that would have come up front with my playing for a factory, but he never said anything. Ma was less pleased. She hadn't realized the degree to which baseball had taken over my life and decided she was going to take more of an interest in my education. An avid reader and a big fan of libraries for as long as I can remember, she started bringing home works by

African-American writers and insisting I read them. I didn't know there were any. None appeared in my high school anthology. Ma introduced me to poets like Countee Cullen and Langston Hughes and writers like Nella Larson and Zora Neale Hurston.

I introduced Sweets. We would read to each other on the back porch when the weather was good and there were no games to be played. Our favorite story was "The Gilded Six-Bits." The husband and wife reminded us of us. Or at least how we felt then and how we always wanted to be. We read it so many times we even took parts and acted them out. The dialogue, which captured on paper the voices of black people, was a favorite. Even if their Southern accents were tough getting used to and we had to practice to get the pronunciation right, we could tell they were real. That made the story even more real.

Joe and Missie May Banks are poor. He works the night shift in a fertilizer factory, and she keeps their house. They aren't the sharpest crayons in the box, but they showed Sweets and me a way to express our love that we hadn't known about. They pretended not to love each other but at the same time were saying how much they really did love each other. "Missie May," take yo' hand out mah pocket!" Joe shouts at his wife. "Ah bet its candy kisses," she replies. "Taint," Joe says. "Woman ain't go no business in a man's clothes nohow. Go way."

They also wrestled. Until we read how Missie May tore through Joe's pockets to find the candy kisses she

knew he'd hidden there for her, Sweets and I were always very gentle with each other. We thought that was
how you were supposed to be when you were in love.
Now we knew we could chase each other around the oak
in the backyard, tickle one another, and even roll on the
grass if we didn't disturb the neighbors. Pa couldn't believe his eyes. "Don't you go doin' nothin' to hurt that
tire," he'd shout at us from the back porch. Ma was also
a little startled, but after we explained we were playing Joe and Missie May from "The Gilded Six-Bits," she
went back to her pile of laundry. As long as what we
were doing came from a story by Zora Neale Hurston,
we could do no wrong.

One day a fellow called Otis Slemmons comes to
the poverty-stricken town in the story. He's got fancy
clothes and a lot of talk about all the places he's been
and people he knows. Missie May isn't impressed: "His
mouf is cut cross-ways, ain't it? Well, he kin lie jes' lak
anybody else." But Joe is. "You womens sho is hard to
sense into things," he tells her. "He's got a five-dollar
gold piece for a stick-pin and he got a ten-dollar gold
piece on his watch chain and his mouf is jes' crammed
full of gold teethes. Sho wisht it was mine. And whut
make it so cool, he got money 'cumulated. And womens
give it all to 'im."

The next thing you know Joe comes home early
from work and catches his wife with Slemmons. Missie May claims she was just trying to get some of the
gold coins Slemmons promised her. She says she wanted
the money for Joe because she saw how much it meant

to him. Joe sends Slemmons somersaulting through the kitchen and out the back door, but the damage has been done. Joe doesn't speak to Missie May for months. She thinks of leaving him, but she can't bring herself to do it. And he can't stay angry with her either. Their love is too strong to be broken. By the end of the story, Slemmons' gold turns out to be false, the Banks are celebrating the arrival of their newborn child, and Missie May is looking forward to the day she can lock Joe in a rough and tumble.

What a difference between this story and those written by the white writers in my literature anthology! For people like F. Scott Fitzgerald and Ernest Hemingway, money was always the ruin of love and sometimes talent. Robert Frost wasn't so keen on it either. It was like Slemmons' false gold. Buy into it, and your dream life quickly becomes a nightmare. Hurston gave me and Sweets hope for our future in ways the white authors didn't. She taught us that relationships may not be perfect, but true love is. If you cherish it and protect it and trust in it, it really can conquer all. Or at least anything money has to offer. The Industrial League could wait. So could the Negro leagues. What was important now was wrestling and candy kisses.

IX

JOHNNY

I'm not saying I was a better player than Bunny. In his first year at Tech, he had the highest batting average, got the most hits, drew the most walks, stole the most bases, and scored more runs than anyone else in the league. He also hit twice as many homers as everyone else on his team combined.

In center field, which is where he roamed when he wasn't on the mound, Bunny was just as impressive. With a man on third and only one out against Chicopee, he ran down a blooping bouncer between first base and right field, changed direction outside the foul line, and threw the runner out as he slid into home. Then there was the triple play against East Longmeadow that started with his over-the-shoulder catch running away from the plate at full speed. Reporters from the *Springfield Daily News* wrote for the next two days about how fast Bunny was and how far he could throw without ever realizing he'd misjudged the ball. If he hadn't stepped toward the diamond when the ball first came off the bat, he never would've had to run after it like he did.

Did I mention Bunny not only went undefeated as a pitcher, he struck out sixteen players in one game? High school baseball games are only seven innings long! Sounds impressive if you didn't know he made his mark against the worst team in Western Massachusetts. Lowly Ludlow.

Which brings me to my point. I may have a lost a few games, but I played on a team with a losing record. There's big difference between being a winning pitcher on a losing team and the best pitcher on a team that wins every game by an average of five runs. And I might have batted over .300 too if all the teams we played hadn't been able to pitch around me. The only strikes I saw were in places nobody could hit them.

So, yes, I was happy Coach Steere asked me to pitch for the American Legion team—I'd worked hard to earn that spot—but he also made it clear that I wasn't going to be competing with Bunny. Unless he suffered an injury or was too tired to pitch, he was Post 21's go-to guy for every game.

It was unfair, but what could I do? If I didn't agree, I wouldn't be on the team, and if I wasn't on the team, I wouldn't get a chance to play, and if I didn't get a chance to play, I wouldn't have an opportunity to show what I could do with real fielders behind me instead of stiffs.

Our captain Tony King told me to keep practicing as if I was going to start every game. When my chance came, even if it was in relief, I had to be at my best. Scouts from the Industrial League and sometimes the

Yankees would be there. They were the ones I wanted to impress even if some of them had come only to see Bunny.

Our first four games were shutouts, and Bunny pitched every one of them from beginning to end. "I'll win every time you let me start," I told Coach Steere after the first game of a double header, "but I can't pitch from the dugout." The words had leapt out of my mouth before I could stop them. Coach only smiled, but I could tell what few wheels he had in his head were already starting to turn. The next thing I knew Bunny was growing a beard in center field.

"You sure you want to start rather than relieve Bunny after we've built you a lead?" Coach asked me as I walked toward the mound.

I just nodded my head. If I'd answered, he would've known from my voice how nervous I was. Warming pine is not the best way to build a player's confidence.

"Play ball!" the umpire shouted.

Up stepped the world's shortest batter. His strike zone was smaller than the tire hanging from the tree in my backyard. The tire! If I could keep my pitches inside its rim, I wouldn't have to worry about who was at the plate.

Four pitches later, leadoff was on the bench.

All afternoon I pretended to throw at different sides of that rim. Not one ball got out of the infield. Then, in the bottom of the fifth, Tony King singled and slid safely into third on a grounder through the middle of the infield by Bunny. Kaiser Lombardi cleaned up with a towering shot over the left field fence, and the game was all but over. That's how the other team felt too. All I had to do was go through the motions for two more innings. When my teammates congratulated me after I struck out the last batter, I felt as if I'd been preparing for Easthampton all my life.

Coach was pleased too. Now he knew I was a lot better than my stats at Cathedral. Once again, I could see wheels rotating behind his eyes. With two great pitchers, he wouldn't have to rely so much on Bunny. He might even be able to compete for the Massachusetts State Championship. No team from Springfield had ever taken that title. Not even the one with Leo Durocher.

X
DANNY

There are fifteen players on the Post 21 team and none of them contributes less than you. You never get to bat, and the only time you play in the field is when the game is all but over and Tony pretends he's tired or hurt and asks Coach to let you take his place at second. You don't mind. You can't grip a bat well enough to place a ball, and you know you'd have trouble holding on to some of the blasts you've seen hit to third and short. That missing tip of the middle finger on your right hand doesn't help your throwing accuracy either. Truth be told, you prefer practices to games. You enjoy the easy camaraderie that takes place among the players when they don't have to think about winning. When the game starts, the fun ends. At least for you. Most players would say the opposite. Nothing beats winning like winning.

You've never been on a team with an African-American, and you wonder what it must be like for him. You're not so stupid as to ask Bunny to touch his hair—others did that and you saw in his eyes how he felt about it—but you'd like to know if he felt differently from the

others in the places within himself that can't be seen
from the outside. You can't tell anything by his behavior because on the surface he acts like everyone else. And
he hardly ever talks. When you do ask him a question,
you often aren't able to tell from his answer whether
he's serious or putting you on. Like the time you wanted
to know why he wasn't stealing as many bases for Post
21 as he had for Tech.

"Too busy scoring runs."

When you followed with a question about how he
got to be so fast, he looked at you like you were swinging
with the wrong end of the bat. You didn't take the hint;
you tried to make a joke of it: "Were you born that way
or did you spend a lot of time running away from people
when you were a kid?"

"The Underground Railroad."

"You worked on a train?"

"My ancestors escaped from slavery on the Underground Railroad. They had to run from one secret loca-
tion to the next. Their speed is in my bones."

Just the opposite of Tony. He never made you feel
stupid. If you complimented him on a good catch or a
clutch hit, he'd say he'd been lucky so you wouldn't lose
confidence in your own abilities. He made you feel like
whatever he could do, you could do it too if you just
worked a little harder in practice, tried a little harder on
the field, and were willing to take the risks you needed
to take if you wanted to win. That's the kind of person
he was. Whenever you talked with him, you came away

feeling good about yourself. And Bunny's breaking all the records Tony had set the year before didn't change that. He couldn't have been very happy about seeing his name erased in so many categories on the Wall of Fame at American Legion Hall, but he never let on how much and was always the first person to congratulate Bunny whenever another of his records fell. He meant every word he said too. That's the way he was. You could tell.

XI
JOHNNY

Post 21 took the Legion League title with twelve wins and one loss—my only bad outing against a team I should have dominated. I could've used some help at the plate, but that's over now. Win or lose, you've got to put every played game behind you. It's the one to come that counts. Fortunately, we'd already qualified for the Massachusetts State Championship. In the opening contest of that series, Bunny struck out nine and allowed only three hits. Springfield 2; Lowell 0. Worcester was next. Bunny held them to two hits and scored the winning run when Jimmy Lawler knocked him home from second. I had to admit he really was the better pitcher. There was no one who could hit like him either. Not before or since.

Then came the New England Championship in St. Albans, Vermont. None of us had ever been so far from Springfield. It took four hours to get there by bus. By the time we arrived, we were as stiff as boards. That didn't stop Bunny. It didn't even slow him down. He shut out Maine that afternoon and hit two home runs.

The following morning he repeated his performance at the plate while pitching us to a four-hit, 17 to 0 romp over New Hampshire. And the scores Bunny prevented were just as impressive. He even picked off a runner at third. How many times have you seen a pitcher do that?

Danny Keyes finally got into a game where he was allowed to swing a bat, coming through with a slow roller that somehow bounced off the first baseman's glove and ended up under the stands for a ground-rule double. No one had ever seen him so excited. When he scored, the whole bench emptied to welcome him home.

The next game was mine. The championship. I was picked to start because Bunny had thrown every inning in our first two contests without a full day's rest in between and no more than two hours separating us from our last game and a team that was playing its first game of the day. We suspected the good legionnaires of St. Albans had scheduled it that way, but what could we do? We were in their backyard.

Coach Steere figured Bunny could rest his arm in center field, and if I got into trouble, he would come in to relieve me. My job, as he so elegantly put it, was to keep Bunny off the mound for as long as I could. He also reminded me I had eight champion fielders backing me up. I didn't have to do everything myself. Talk about a pep talk! You'd think I was pitching from a wheelchair. I decided not to let what he said bother me. If we won, we'd be heading for the Eastern Regionals in Gastonia, North Carolina. I'd never heard of the place and didn't have a clue where it might be, but I was determined to be the reason we got there.

It wasn't easy. The Vermont pitcher turned out to be the toughest we'd faced all summer. A six-foot, four-inch, left-handed knuckleballer who weighed more than two hundred pounds. No one had ever seen anyone like him. Or anything like a knuckleball. Even Bunny was impressed. That catamount held us scoreless for eleven innings. No one—not Tony, not Bunny, not Jimmy, not Kaiser, not anybody—could connect against him our first time through the order. Not the second time neither. Not even to tip a ball foul and extend the at bat. One inning we'd all be swinging ahead of the pitch, and the next inning we'd all go down after it was in the catcher's mitt. Half the time we didn't even know where the ball was. Even their catcher had trouble following and holding on to it. And the odd thing was the roundster never looked so big. It was as if all we had to do was put some wood on it and it would be gone.

But knuckleballs don't work like that. They leave the pitcher's hand in one direction and then float in several others between the mound and the plate. You can't tell where it's going, and you can only guess where it will end up. The harder you try to hit it, the more unlikely the chances that you will, and the more frustrated you become when you don't. When one of us was finally lucky enough to make contact, the ball traveled neither far nor fast. We looked more like a team of dribblers than state champions.

But I was just as tough for just as long, giving up four harmless singles and a walk.

In the bottom of the eleventh, Green Mountain Boy on the Mound must have tired. I got our first solid hit: a line drive that flew between first and second base. Bunny then moved me to third with his first swing, and before another pitcher could warm up, Kaiser sent me home with a blast down the first base line. The Vermonters knew the game was over as soon as they heard the crack of the bat. Their right fielder didn't even bother to go after the ball.

It was the best game I would ever play. No one in American Legion history had pitched eleven straight innings. I remember every strikeout as if it were yesterday. I even went so far as to retrieve the ball Kaiser had stroked to win the game. It was lying in the grass waiting for me. Everyone on the team signed it. Even Joe Carmody, our mascot. That ball sat on my desk the entire time I served with the state legislature in Boston. And how many times have I replayed in my mind's eye the hit that put me in position to score the winning run! It's the highlight of my life. That and crossing the plate to become the Champions of New England. Absolutely nothing compares. Not then, not now, not ever.

XII
BUNNY

Ma and Pa agreed: North Carolina was no place for a colored boy. Especially one who'd never heard of Jim Crow. Did I know I couldn't buy a stamp at a white's only window in the post office or check out a book in a white's only library? Did I know I could be arrested for drinking water from the same fountain, using the same toilet, and sitting at the same lunch counter as a white person? I wasn't even allowed to play checkers with a white person in a public park.

Sweets said it could be worse. Her grandfather had moved his family from South Carolina after he found work at the Springfield Armory during World War I. They were part of the Great Migration that you never read about in history books. She knew from the stories he told what happened to colored people visiting from the North who weren't aware of Southern customs: "What if the next time I see you, you're on a postcard swinging from a lamppost because you looked a white woman in the eye while asking directions?"

I heard, but I was too excited to listen. My first time out of Massachusetts was when the Post 21 team traveled to St. Albans. Now we were going all the way to North Carolina. I couldn't wait to test myself against players from other parts of the country, especially Florida where baseball was said to be played at a higher level because games there could be scheduled all year long. I found Gastonia on a map, but I had no sense of how far away it was from Massachusetts or how long it would take us to get there or what the people would be like when we arrived.

First we had to leave. Ma and Pa together didn't make $18 a week. The trip to Gastonia would cost several times that. With Post 21 in danger of elimination before a pitch was thrown, the people of Springfield stepped up to the collection plate and within days batted in enough money to pay the expenses of the entire team. Talk about a home run! There was even enough left over to buy jackets and ties for the players who didn't have them.

I couldn't let my teammates down now even if I wanted to stay. The people of Springfield were counting on me too. And if my parents and Sweets were right, there was more at stake than a baseball game. "You're going to discover some of the reasons our people fled the South," Sweets told me before I climbed aboard the train at Union Station. Pa's last words were also foreboding: "Remember you is a human being that knows how to act like a human being even when you isn't being treated as a human being." Then Ma added, "And don't you let nobody drag you down to their level. You try to get back at them and you be just as bad as they." What a send-off!

And what a ride! In a Pullman no less. I'd seen the interior of trains in some of the movies shown at Kelleher's Garage, but this was the first time I was ever on one. We had seats with pillows, beds with reading lights, and a wood-paneled dining car with a written menu. Real plates and silverware too. Not only that but the food was hot. Even at lunchtime. If this was what travel was like in the Negro leagues, you could sign me up right now!

When the American Legion team from Cumberland, Maryland, boarded the train in Washington, we got to see how we looked back in Springfield. We showed them how to open the windows, pull the foot rests out from under the seats, and turn down the card tables as if we'd been riding trains all our lives. After storing their luggage in the sleeping car, the Crabs, as we were already calling them, returned to sit with the Beans even though we told them we weren't from Boston. They said they didn't live anywhere near the ocean either.

I sat in a seat by the window. Several of the newcomers looked confused when they saw me sitting in the car, but no one said anything. A few others squeezed into seats with their teammates rather than take the empty one next to me. Two different conductors then asked me to show them my ticket without asking anyone else. I didn't get it at first, but when I did, I was neither hurt nor angry. After listening to my parents and Sweets,

I'd expected to be moved to the mail car. Or thrown off the train at the next stop. Possibly even arrested. If this was the worst Jim Crow could do to make me feel uncomfortable, he wasn't nearly as powerful as people made him out to be. I would have no trouble behaving like a human being. Besides, I wasn't going to Gastonia to make friends, and North Carolina was still a part of the United States of America. The only place on earth where all men are created equal. As long as I had a paid-for ticket, there was nothing anyone could do about it. That night, as I undressed for bed, I looked up at a full moon reassuring me I was right and within my rights. It was surrounded by three circles: red, white, and blue. The American flag was smiling down at me.

XIII
DANNY

23 August 1934. The train pulls in right on schedule. The sun is already shining and there's not a cloud in the sky. No baseball ever saw a brighter day.

Neither have you. A band on the platform outside your window plays songs from what could only be the South. It seems like every third or fourth one is "Dixie." The team from Maryland is soon off the train and into a bus heading for the Armitage Hotel. You're still in your seat. Mr. Sid Harris, the Commander of Post 21 and now the team's manager, tells anyone not too excited to listen that we're more than just ballplayers: "Each and every one of you is an ambassador from the North. Everywhere you go, whatever you do, people will judge New England by the way you behave. It's very important to leave the people here with the best possible impression."

Because your stump with a thumb doesn't allow you to move quickly with your bags, you wait in your seat for everyone else to get off the train. You see it all from the height advantage of your window. A trumpet player nudges the fellow playing next him and motions toward the players getting off the train. Both take their horns from their lips. More nudges follow and more instruments are silenced. At least one horn is already on its way into its case before the conductor notices his band is falling apart before his eyes. He searches around him for an explanation. When one doesn't appear, he looks back to the band for help. No one says a word. Everyone is packing and leaving. The conductor then turns inquisitively toward the train. A saddened look, like a dark cloud appearing just before a storm, spreads across his brow. He lowers his baton to his side. His answer is standing on the platform.

It's Bunny. He notices the band has stopped playing but seems to be unaware of the reason. So is everyone else on the team. Mr. Harris and Coach Steere don't have a clue either; they're too busy lining up bags of baseball equipment by the street side of the platform. You join your teammates, but you don't say anything because you think you might be mistaken about the meaning behind what you saw. When the bus from the hotel pulls up beside the platform, you discover that you weren't.

The driver hops out, points to Bunny, and orders him to start loading the equipment bags onto the bus. Bunny doesn't move. He looks as if he's not sure he heard the man correctly even though everyone knows he has. "Did you hear me, boy?" the driver shouts. "I said pick up those bags and be quick about it."

Bunny puts down his suitcase and begins to do what he's been told. Mr. Harris stops him. "This young man is a member of the team," he tells the driver.

Now it's the driver's turn to wear the same look as the conductor of the band; only his puzzlement is momentary. He climbs back into his bus, shuts the door, and pulls away from the station before anyone can hop aboard. Welcome to Gastonia!

XIV
BUNNY

Asked to show my train ticket as if my seat had to have been issued by mistake was amusing. The second time it happened, I couldn't help but smile at how hard the conductor tried to find an error on that little piece of paper. He turned it over and over in his hands three times. Front and back, front and back, front and back. Nothing.

Watching the band disperse the minute I stepped onto the station platform was hurtful. The despairing way the musicians shook their heads as they peeled away from the group made me feel as if they thought I was not only ignorant of the offense I'd caused but too dense to understand what I'd done even if it was explained to me. The conductor looked at me as if to ask how I could have been so inconsiderate as to ruin his perfectly fine rendition of "Sewanee River." I tried to convince myself that none of this had anything to do with me, but it had. It had everything to do with me.

Ordered to load bags onto the bus was worse still. I was embarrassed. Not because I minded helping out but because the driver assumed I couldn't possibly be there for any other reason. Here I was probably the biggest, strongest, fastest athlete ever to come out of Western Massachusetts, and in Gastonia I was only good enough to make life easier for white people. Now I knew what Ma must have felt like when she did white people's laundry. How often must she have looked at our house needing to be cleaned or food waiting to be prepared but had to finish washing their clothes and hang them on the line before she could tend to her own family. I could only imagine how Pa must have felt. So proud of his ancestors and his blacksmith name, he could do no better for himself than chauffer white people who had nothing better to do with themselves than sit in the back seat of a car he would never be able to afford. No wonder he called the house he worked out of a plantation.

When Coach Steere and Mr. Harris divided the equipment among us and we each carried a share along with our bags to the hotel, I felt responsible. If I hadn't been there, everyone would have ridden in the bus. They wouldn't have had to carry anything. What was happening now was no longer just about me. That I could handle. When you've been booed by fans as many times as I have, it takes more than a crummy band or a stupid bus driver to turn your head. The thing about opposing fans is they don't really hate you; they just hate what you're doing to their team. When that hate motivates you to do more of what already has made them so irate, and you succeed in spite of their team's efforts to stop you, you gain their respect. This wasn't like that. This was personal. Tony, Danny, Kaiser, Johnny and the rest of the Post 21 team were being punished because I was one of them.

The empty bus was parked in front of the hotel entrance when we arrived. It was impossible not to notice. So was the message it sent.

XV
BUNNY

"We got a law here that says no niggers can sleep in no hotels for white people."

I'd heard the word before, but I never heard anyone say it like that. It was as if the hotel manager was talking about some kind of vermin that white people needed to be protected from. Get too close to me and you'd be sure to come down with a terrible disease.

"I've never heard of such a law," Mr. Harris told the hotel manager.

"You ain't never been in North Carolina."

Fifteen players stood listening while Mr. Harris and the hotel manager discussed the law. I felt humiliated. I wasn't good enough to stay in the Armitage Hotel even though my room had been paid for. What did they think I was going to do? Dirty the sheets? Forget to flush the toilet? Not drain the tub? I recalled my parents' advice about dealing with Jim Crow: remember to behave like a human being and don't let anyone drag you down to their level. What did they mean? What was I supposed to do?

"We've arranged for your boy to stay with the local nigger doctor."

"Mr. Taliaferro will stay with the team." This was the first time anyone ever referred to me in this way. I felt as if Mr. Harris was restoring some of my dignity. The feeling didn't last long.

"Don't you think your boy will be better off with his own kind?"

"He is with his own kind."

"Please be reasonable, Mr. Harris. If you were a guest in a foreign country, wouldn't you respect the local customs even if you didn't agree with all of them?"

"We're not in a foreign country."

"You're far enough away from Massachusetts not to have much choice."

"The Armitage is the only hotel in Gastonia?"

"Unless you fancy sleeping with niggers. It's the same wherever you go. The law applies to all. We couldn't change it if we wanted to."

Mr. Harris demanded to see the American Legion representative in charge of the tournament.

I told Coach Steere I didn't want to cause any trouble.

"You're not the one causing trouble," he replied.

Mr. Harris overheard what we said and turned his back on the front desk. "Bunny, you are a member of this team," he told me. "Where it goes, you go."

The team didn't look like it was going anywhere. Some of the players shuffled their feet to relieve the boredom of having to wait for their rooms. Others looked at the clock in the lobby and then at me as if it was my fault their time was being wasted. I didn't look back. I couldn't. I knew I was responsible for how they felt, though I did take some comfort in knowing the color of my skin prevented them from seeing the shame pulsating beneath its surface.

Nobody saying a word to me was worse than the stares. It was as if the hotel wouldn't provide anyone seen talking to me with a room either. Contamination by association. Even the fellows I had known before the team was formed were becoming impatient. It was getting hot, we were getting hungry, and Mr. Harris was getting nowhere with the hotel manager.

"I don't mind sleeping with the doctor's family," I told Coach Steere.

"Well, I do," Mr. Harris shot back.

While waiting for the American Legion official, Mr. Harris gave each player his one dollar daily expense allowance. He told the team to grab some lunch in town, have a look around, and be back at the hotel in two hours. Our bags would be in our rooms. We were to pick up our keys at the front desk, change into our uniforms, and meet in the lobby at one o'clock.

All except me. While the other bags were being carried to pre-assigned rooms, I had to wait with mine and Mr. Harris for the official in charge of the games. It was then I discovered what grown men do when they don't want to talk about what they know they should be talking about. Neither of us said a word.

XVI
BUNNY

Happy Feller was how he introduced himself. A bank manager by day, he looked like the kind of person who made up for too many hours behind a desk with too many bottles of beer after he got out of work. His eyes were watery, his face was flushed, his neck hid his shirt collar, his suspenders ran down his sides, his stomach rested on the waist of his pants, and his feet looked as if they'd been stuffed into his shoes. The first man I'd ever seen chew tobacco, he said he didn't want the "situation to get out of hand" and promised to "set things right."

"The law regarding niggers staying in hotels reserved for white people can't possibly include servants," Mr. Feller told the manager. "It would be too much of an inconvenience. Why don't we just register the boy as the team's servant?"

"Because he's not."

"That will be our little secret," Mr. Feller replied as he discretely slid a thin envelope across the front desk.

"He'll have to sleep on a cot. We can't have no nigger sleeping in no bed for white people."

Mr. Feller agreed.

"And the boy will have to stay in the same room as Mr. Harris who has to promise to make him sleep on the cot. I don't want to lose my job."

Mr. Harris agreed.

"And he'll have to be seen performing all the duties of a servant. Especially when he's in the lobby. He'll have to carry everyone's equipment and load it onto the bus all by himself. He'll also have to hold open the lobby door for the coaches, his teammates, and any other white people who want to pass through. When the team checks out, he'll have to carry and load its luggage. Under no circumstances can anyone mistake the nigger for a guest."

XVII
JOHNNY

Gastonia wasn't nearly as large as Springfield. It didn't look as old neither. And from what Danny and I could see, there wasn't much to what there was. A church with two yellow windows and no steeple, a main street covered with dust, and some kind of mill you could hear humming in the distance. It was only ten miles from Charlotte, but Gastonia seemed to be so cut off from anything worthwhile it was almost lonesome.

At midday, the town was practically empty. Except for a perspiring man, whose suspenders seemed to be holding up more than his pants, and an elderly black man who stepped off the curb to let us pass, nothing moved. No children's voices could be heard. The sun burned fiery hot and the sky was as bright as glass. Unless you had someplace to go, there was absolutely nothing to do.

Except perhaps eat. Two run-down diners, their exteriors white with glare from the sun, competed to satisfy the appetites of fifteen hungry boys. The prices were right at both. A coffee and two doughnuts went for eight cents. Two cents cheaper than in Springfield. Chicken pie sold for five cents. That was four cents cheaper. Everything except the newspaper cost less. At two cents, that was the same. You could go a long way on a dollar in Gastonia.

The same couldn't be said for much else. Over soggy grilled-cheese sandwiches and water-downed Cokes, Danny and I talked about what was happening to Bunny. We said how terrible it all was and how lucky we were not to live in a place like Gastonia. Even the name was ugly. Like the place was made out of gas or something. I kept to myself my hope that the whites-only rule at the hotel would also be applied at the ballpark. After my big win in Vermont, I wanted the opportunity to pitch my team into the national finals. I wanted to play baseball in Chicago.

Danny and I decided to check out Main Street before returning to the hotel. It wasn't more than a few hundred yards long. We were wondering what it must be like to live in such a dreary place when three boys, all older than us, stepped out of an alleyway.

"Well, what have we here?"

"I do believe it's two of them nigger lovers."

"I do believe you're right."

"You been keeping us waiting."

"We was about to think we needed an appointment."

"Don't you know it's rude to keep your betters waiting?"

"Where did you learn your manners?"

"You two could do with a lesson in courtesy."

The boys wore tee shirts with the sleeves cut off. Muscles bulged from their arms and they had no necks. The one that seemed to be the leader had a spread of teeth resembling the stained keys of a piano which hasn't been played in years. All spoke with protruding lower jaws as if daring us to make something, anything, of what they said. They were just itching for a fight.

"What have you got against us?" Danny asked plaintively. "We've never done anything to you."

"So you say," the biggest boy answered.

"Why not the nigger?" I heard myself saying. "Why pick on us when he's the one you want?"

Suddenly, the hot town froze. No one moved. Nothing happened. No sound was made. A shadow had crossed the distance between us and the townies. We all turned to look. It was Bunny. I knew he'd heard what I said. There was no way he couldn't have.

"We ain't got no quarrel with you," the one with the yellow teeth told him.

Bunny stepped between me and Danny. He didn't even look at us. He punched the one who'd spoken smack full in the face without saying a word. The bully stumbled back, his legs stiffened by the blow, his eyes widened by the shock. A second bully stepped forward to defend his buddy; Bunny sent him to the ground with a blow to the side of his head. When the third boy saw blood pouring from the nose of the first, he turned and ran before Bunny could lay a hand on him. The fellow on the ground rolled over and looked into my eyes without ever seeing me. He knew he was hurt but was too stunned to know how badly. The other one looked like he wasn't aware of having been hurt. He didn't even grab his nose to try to stop the bleeding.

Bunny didn't say anything. He just turned and walked toward the hotel.

XVIII
DANNY

Elysian Fields. You know it from the mythology course you took at Classical as a kind of paradise for dead Greeks. Only this Elysian Fields is no heaven on earth. It's the name of a ballpark in Gastonia that holds more people than have come to all the games you've played this summer put together. Perhaps as many as three thousand. And the place is packed. But these fans haven't turned up during the hottest part of a sweltering day to watch a baseball game. They've come to witness a practice.

And make a statement. Before a single Massachusetts player can take the field, they're booing and cursing and making so much noise stomping their feet against the wooden bleachers you can hardly make out what any one of them is saying. Still, some of the messages do get through. They call you "nigger" and "nigger lover" and "Yankee trash." They threaten to tear the uniform off the back of any player who leaves the dugout. They tell you you've already played your last game of the season. They order you back to New England where they say you belong. They warn that the Ku Klux Klan will kidnap you from your hotel room in the middle of the night. They say your parents will never know what happened to you, but you'll be too dead to care. "Take a good look at that there diamond, boys," an usher announces as he walks by the dugout. "It's the lass one you all is evah goin' to see."

XIX

JOHNNY

Danny hasn't spoken to me since Bunny clobbered those punks. When I sit next to him in the dugout after the team has taken the field for practice, he moves away. Not far enough for any of the other subs to sense something is wrong but far enough that I'll notice. And know the reason too. How could I not? It's what I said just before Bunny rescued us from a beat down. It's the word I used.

I keep telling myself I didn't mean it the way Danny thinks, but what other way could it have been meant? I thought of telling him what I really meant was the two of us were no match for those bullies. With Bunny we stood a better chance of getting back to the hotel in one piece. He was more their size. "You see, Danny, with Bunny on our side those toughs would've been afraid to fight because they knew we would've beaten them. If I'd called Bunny by his name, they would've thought I wasn't taking them seriously. I had to say a word they'd understand." I also thought of talking to Bunny. "You see, Bunny, those thugs really wanted to fight a colored guy, not us. That's why I said what I did. It had nothing to do with you personally." But I couldn't convince myself that either Danny or Bunny would believe me. I didn't even believe me. They heard what I'd said and they knew what I'd meant.

Now it's Bunny's turn to say what he means in the best way he knows how. With his bat. He's been listening to obscenities, insults, and threats since we got off the train. Coach Steere has told him not to leave the dugout until the team is on the field. The plan is for Bunny to take his swings before anyone else, return to the dugout, and watch the rest of the practice from the bench. Coach sees no reason to get the locals more riled up than they already are.

The roar they make when Bunny steps onto the field is more ominous than anything we've heard. Not just the words but the sound. It's almost as if some kind of evil spirit has taken possession of the people's souls. How else can you explain their behavior? Our mascot, Joe Carmody, starts to cry. So does Franny Luce. Joe Kelly makes the sign of the cross. The closer Bunny gets to the plate the louder the noise becomes. You can't even hear the plane that's checking out the action from above. Rotten fruit fills the air as he approaches the batter's box. A few tomatoes too. If Bunny notices any of this, he doesn't let on. To what extent it bothers him, you can't tell. It's almost as if the crowd isn't even there. It's just him and the ball and his bat.

Coach Steere throws his first pitch right down the pike, and Bunny sends it special delivery over the left field fence. Two hundred and eighty feet are covered in just a few seconds. That shuts the crowd up, but only for a moment. Anyone who has just come back to their seat with a hot dog or was talking to a neighbor when Bunny first stepped up to the plate is now screaming their lungs out.

Bunny silences them again on the coach's next pitch. Mark this one at three hundred and twenty feet. Right over the center field fence.

Coach's third pitch also clears the outfield fence. The Gastonians have never seen anything like it. So many half-eaten hot dogs take off from the seats they almost block out the sun. The whole stadium shakes from the stomping. Even the bench in the dugout trembles. Danny couldn't talk to me now if he wanted to. The noise is that loud.

Bunny's not concerned. He's already found the rhythm that enables him to relax and at the same time swing hard at each ball Coach Steere throws. What is it that white people have been saying about black people not being able to compete when the pressure is on? Somebody neglected to tell Bunny. Now he's doing to the Gastonians with his bat what the Gastonians couldn't do to him with their behavior. They wouldn't let him forget he's black, and he's not going to let them forget it either. Not for a very long time. Every ball that crosses the plate winds up in Gastonia. Six home runs on six pitches.

XX
DANNY

You never got out of the dugout let alone on to the field. Coach Steere called off practice before you had a chance. And not just because he ran out of baseballs. The crowd started throwing drained Coke bottles, empty tin cans, even small rocks. The weight of these items enabled those nearest the field to cover the distance that prevented their half-eaten food from reaching any of the players. Bunny was now in danger. So were those in positions near either sideline.

You listen to the sound of trash bouncing off the roof of the dugout. You see it piling up on the field in front of you. The people of Gastonia don't realize it, but they've just handed Bunny another victory. Perhaps his greatest. He's reduced them to having to resort to violence to stop him from blasting baseballs out of their ballpark. The booing didn't do it, the stomping didn't do it, the name-calling didn't do it, and the threats didn't do it. The baseball team from Gastonia wasn't even given an opportunity to do it.

You think Bunny would be pleased, but he's sitting in the dugout with the same expressionless face he wore when he saved you and Johnny from getting beaten up by those creeps. He didn't say anything then either. If you didn't know better, you'd think it was the top of the ninth with two outs and Post 21 was up by ten runs.

Suddenly the jeers turn to cheers. The hotel bus has pulled up just outside the visitor's bullpen. The team from Maryland gets out, and the driver helps them with their bags. Their turn to practice is now your chance to escape. Coach Steere orders everyone to tie their gloves to their belts. He wants all hands free to swing the bats he's distributing from the equipment bags. Anything other than gloves, bats, and what's already in the pockets of our uniforms is to be left behind.

Coach says Bunny will break from the dugout first because he has the best chance of reaching the bus before being hit with something, but Bunny insists on protecting the rear along with Tony and Kaiser Lombardi. He says he got us into this mess and now it's his job to help get us out. Coach doesn't argue with him. There's no time. Little Joe Carmody will now go first and no one will run ahead of him. "We're a team," Coach says. "We stick together no matter what."

The fans are so surprised to see us bursting from the dugout you'd think Bunny had hit another home run. They not only stop hurling projectiles, they forget to boo. Off the playing field and through an opening in the bleachers before anyone can think to stop us, we pass the bus's driver walking with the coach from the

Maryland team. "You all keep on goin' 'til you reach Massachusetts!" he shouts. "An don't come back anytime soon," the coach adds, "you heah?"

You and Johnny hoist Carmody onto Coach Steere's shoulders. He squeezes through an open window in the bus and discovers the door is already unlocked. Your teammates pile in. Coach jumps behind the wheel. The key is waiting in the ignition. "Time to go," he yells to Bunny, Tony, and Kasier. They're threatening with their bats the fans who were fast enough to catch up with us.

"Call him a 'nigger,'" Tony shouts at them. "Go ahead. Do it now. See what happens."

You wonder what could possibly be making him say this. Aren't these people angry enough already?

"Just call him one," Tony continues. "I want to see which one of you bastards has the nerve to say it where I can see you."

"We don't take no orders from no Yankee trash," someone replies.

"I'm not ordering you, you coward. I'm daring you. Call him a 'nigger.' See what you got coming."

Tony raises his bat and takes a step toward the fellow who spoke, but Bunny and Kaiser grab him by the shoulders. The three back onto the bus, and the door closes behind them. What protects the players, however, also protects the fans. They surge forward and try to tip the bus over by rocking it. Others let air out of the tires. Rocks fly through several windows. Coach Steere pulls away before someone gets hurt. At least not a hurt anyone can see.

XXI
BUNNY

The teams from Maryland and Florida have announced they won't play against Massachusetts if I'm allowed on the field, the hotel manager has informed Mr. Harris that Post 21 will not be allowed in the banquet room at tonight's welcoming dinner if I'm with the team, and the same American Legion official who arranged for me to be the players' servant and sleep on a cot says the police aren't sure they can protect me from all the fans expected to show up for our first game. Or the Ku Klux Klan. They plan to be there too.

"What if Bunny hits a white player with a pitch?" Happy Feller wants to know. "What if Bunny slides into somebody trying to steal a base?"

"What if Bunny pitches a no-hitter? Mr. Harris retaliates. "What if Bunny knocks in the winning run?"

We change into our jackets and ties and wait in Coach Steere's room to learn our fate, but the players' minds are not on the banquet. They can't stop talking about what happened at the ballpark and how we commandeered the bus to make our escape. It all seems like an adventure to them.

I feel nothing but shame. Those six home runs not only jeopardized my team's chances of playing in the tournament, I let my parents down by behaving in ways they warned me against. Their last words to me before leaving Springfield were to behave like a human being regardless of how I might be treated and not allow myself to be dragged down to the level of anyone who disrespected me by retaliating in kind. I failed to do both.

Worse. I remembered what they'd said and purposely didn't pay them any mind. Maybe if I'd been allowed to enter either of the two diners in Gastonia or at least sit without eating at the same table as my teammates, what happened afterwards might not have happened at all, but I doubt it. I knew exactly what I was doing the whole time. Before I even threw the first punch, I saw it all happen like a movie in my mind's eye. I also knew I wasn't pounding those bullies just because they were taunting two of my teammates. Danny and Johnny weren't in danger. Not really. If those thugs were going to do anything to them, they would've already done it. All their talk was just that. Talk. What I really was doing with my fists was sending a message to Johnny. He was the one who'd called me a "nigger." At least the people in Gastonia are honest about their feelings. You know where you stand with them. Not Johnny. He felt the same way they did, but because he grew up in Massachusetts, he knew better than to say what he did unless it was behind my back. I would've liked to have hit him too, but coach would've been furious. I had to find another way to let Johnny know about what it means to be a member of a team, but because I didn't listen to my parents, I chose the wrong one.

The same is true for what happened at Elysian Fields. Air mailing all those balls out of the park was easy because I'd already imagined what I was going to do while waiting in the dugout. If I'd played it smart, I would've sent a few grounders and pop flies to my teammates and let the people of Gastonia go home with the impression that their team had nothing to fear from me. Then, when I got in a game, I could unload on them all. The team and the fans. But, no, I had to show everybody what I was made of. I had to try to earn their respect by hitting them where I knew I threatened them the most. In the loss column. What was the difference between their throwing all their garbage at me and my hitting all those homeruns when we were both doing what we did for the same reason?

Enter Mr. Harris. He gives it to us straight: "Boys, you've got two choices. You can play without Bunny or you can pack your bags and leave for Springfield. The decision is yours."

XXII
BUNNY

Coach Steere says Tony King should speak first because he's our Captain. Last year, Tony was voted Most Valuable Player; this year, I broke every record he set. That couldn't have set too well with him even though he congratulated me after every mark that fell. Now I wish I'd stopped for a moment to think what it must have been like for him to see his name being replaced at the top of the list in all those categories.

I used to feel sorry for the players on the teams we beat. Especially if the score was close. Why did I never stop to think about the affect my success might be having on my teammates? What harm would it have done to let others share in the glory? What need did I have for all those records? What was I trying to prove? When did it become all about me? Some of those bases I stole for no other reason than I could. Up 13 to 0 against New Hampshire, I was still stealing bags. Every time I got on one, I stole another. Six before the game was half over. Two fewer and Tony would still be holding on to the only record he had left.

Now it's payback time. I won't blame Tony if he'd rather play than go home. He didn't come all the way to Gastonia for the train ride. Now he's got a chance to lead Post 21 to the finals in Chicago and get his name back on the American Legion Wall of Fame at the same time.

"Bunny is member of this team," he tells everyone. "He has as much right to play as anybody. Nobody can tell him he can't. If he doesn't play, I don't either."

"Me neither," says Danny Keyes. "No championship is worth winning if it means playing without Bunny."

"We wouldn't be here if it wasn't for Bunny," adds Kaiser Lombardi. "I say we head for home."

And that's how it goes. There's no debate. Only votes. All the other players—Jimmy Lawler, Franny Luce, Bobby Triggs, Ray O'Shay, Joe Kelly, Franny O'Connell, John Malaguiti, Louis Grondolski, Freddy Laczek, Joe Kogut, even Johnny Coffey—say pretty much the same thing: if I'm not playing, they're not playing.

I feel both bad and good. Bad because I know I'm preventing my teammates from competing in a tournament we worked so hard to reach. Good because my teammates voted to stick by me. They know they have a good chance of winning the Regionals without me, but their decision has nothing to do with my ability as an athlete. For the first time I feel that, play or not play, I'm one of them no matter what the law, the bus driver, the hotel manager, the Legion official, or the people of Gastonia say.

Mr. Harris asks me if there's anything I want to add.

There is: "Coach always says there is no 'I' in the word 'team.' I wanted that championship so bad I could taste it. I can still taste it. Especially after the way those people acted at the ballpark today. But now I know some things are more important than winning. That's having teammates like you. The people here treat me as if I'm some kind of insect. You showed me I'm a human being with the right to be treated like a human being. You're more than teammates. You're the best friends anyone could ever want, and after tonight, I'm the best friend any of you will ever need."

Coach Steere wants to add something: "I'm more proud of this team right now than at any time during the season. Not for what you achieved but for what you chose not to achieve. No bigger champions ever walked on any baseball diamond. Not in my book."

Now it's Mr. Harris's turn, but he's interrupted by a knock on the door. Happy Feller sticks his head in before anyone can open it. "You all gotta get outta here," he tells us. "You're about to be arrested for stealing the hotel's bus!"

XXIII
JOHNNY

Three cars are running their engines outside the kitchen door of the Armitage Hotel. Coach Steere, Mr. Harris, and Mr. Feller each grab an empty front seat and the rest of us jump in behind. Any bags that don't fit in the trunks go on our laps.

We don't know who's driving us or where we're going—it's all dirt roads with sharp turns—but we get there fast. An old plantation? Even with an almost full moon it's hard to tell. But there is a big old white house in the distance and what feels like a loading dock under our feet. Railroad tracks with weeds as tall as Kaiser run alongside. Mr. Feller tells us trains used to stop here to take on cotton bales. Now one is going to stop, pick us up, and get us out of North Carolina before the police realize we haven't headed for Charlotte. That would have been the logical place to go.

Our drivers can't stay until the train arrives. No one knows for sure when that will be. Sometime before daylight. Mr. Feller can't wait either. It's too dangerous. The police may have been momentarily fooled, but the

Ku Klux Klan won't be. Their members are everywhere. Three cars speeding on back roads in the middle of the night can't help but arouse suspicion. If Mr. Feller and his friends are found helping us, they may not live to tell about it. They've got to go, and we've got to wait.

Imagine two adults and fifteen kids standing in the middle of the night on an abandoned platform more than a thousand miles from home with no protection. Their only hope is an unknown train making an unscheduled stop sometime before dawn. What if it's a trick? What if we're never seen again? Every time the headlights of a car flash by, we think the Klan is on its way. What would they do if they caught us? We could all be shot and buried in some mass grave where no one would find us. Or hanged and pictured on a postcard as an example for others who challenge the way life is lived in the South. The mosquitoes don't help either. Their bite is worse than that of either the Klan or the police. So far.

XXIV
BUNNY

No dining car or hot meals on this train. Not even a sandwich. No turned down sleeper beds either. We sit up all the way to New York. Johnny asks Tony if he'll switch seats with him for a few minutes. There's something he wants to tell me. He says he's sorry for what he said on the street in Gastonia. He knows what he did was cowardly. He just didn't want to get hurt. He thought if he called me a "nigger" those bullies wouldn't beat him up. If he hadn't been so scared, he never would've said it.

"Don't worry," I tell him. "I'd probably have done the same thing if I were in your place."

Johnny's relieved. He goes back to his seat thinking I understand how he felt. The truth is I don't. Not really. It seems that no matter how sure you are about what's right or wrong, you can still be made to act differently than you ever thought you would. So much depends on the situation. Ma has been telling me all my life that violence is wrong. It never solves anything and only makes everything worse. That's why she told me never to lower myself to the level of anyone who mistreats me. Once you do that, it's an eye for an eye and a tooth for a tooth and before long everybody is blind and toothless.

If only she'd told Pa. His beating me before he suspected I might have a future in the Industrial League only made me want to hit back, but I couldn't strike out at him. He's my father. I have to obey and respect him. And to hit anyone else would only have gotten me in trouble with Ma. So I made sure the only people I ever hit were wearing helmets and shoulder pads. Shooting baskets and slamming baseballs gave me a similar feeling. It wasn't as intense, but it was there all the same. That may be a big part of why I play sports. They enable me to get even with Pa at someone else's expense. It may also explain why I always feel sorry for the players my teams beat even though I'm happy that we won. I don't want to feel guilty for what I've done to them anymore than Johnny doesn't want to feel guilty for calling me a "nigger."

The need to get even got out of hand almost as soon as we arrived at the hotel. I was so angry at the marching band, the bus driver, and the hotel manager, I wanted to hurt them like they'd hurt me. But what could I do? They weren't wearing baseball uniforms, we weren't on a playing field, and I didn't have a bat or a ball in my hands. I had to wait until our first practice to strike back, but so much happened faster than I had time for. It was almost as if I was following a script that I couldn't change if I wanted to. I was even angry with Mr. Feller for wanting to list me as a servant so I could stay in the hotel with my teammates, and then I got furious at Mr. Harris for agreeing to it even though

I kept my mouth shut at the time. Neither one of them ever thought to ask me how I felt about carrying all the bags and holding the lobby door open for any white people that wanted to pass through. And when my teammates didn't get up and walk out after I wasn't allowed in either of those diners, I wanted to get back at them too. Especially as some of them pretended not to see what was going on. That's the real reason I popped those punks. I wanted to set an example of how my teammates should have behaved when they saw me being discriminated against. I was still setting an example when I sent all those balls special delivery over the fence at Elysian Fields. But once again, I'd chosen the wrong way to send my message. If I hadn't picked up my bat, Tony might not have turned his bat on the crowd that chased after us from the ballpark. My behavior made him want to strike back too, and his made the people of Gastonia feel the same way about us. That's why they tried to turn the bus over while we were in it. Violence begets violence.

All that changed in Coach Steere's room. This time, Tony chose to follow a different kind of example. One he created for himself. Just because the people of Gastonia behaved like animals didn't mean that we had to behave like animals in return. That would only prove them right about us without their ever having to take a look at themselves. Returning to Springfield rather than play without me will send a more powerful message than any home run or punch in the nose that I could ever deliver. It's no wonder he's our Captain.

XXV

DANNY

Penn Station, New York. You weren't in Gastonia for a day, but it seems like a week.

Mr. Harris and Coach Steere are talking about whether to take the team to see a game at Yankee Stadium. The Cleveland Indians are in town. You're a Yankees fan. So is everyone else. Every spring the Bronx Bombers come to Springfield to play their farm team in two exhibition games before the major league season begins. The Ponies never win, but no one expects them to either. You and dozens of other kids watch the first seven innings of each contest through knotholes popped out of the wooden boards that make up the outfield fence. Then, before the first Yankee comes to bat in top of the eighth, you're allowed to take any empty seat in the park. Some kids don't even bother watching the game through the knotholes. They just show up after the seventh inning stretch. When the game is over, dozens of you move onto the field for autographs. Babe Ruth's is the most sought after. It's been seven years since he hit 60 home runs in a single season, but he can still put the ball outside of any park in the American League. Perhaps because he was raised in an orphanage, he doesn't head for the showers until every kid who wants his autograph walks away with one. You've got three.

You'd love to see the Yankees whip the Indians in the house that Ruth built, but you can't help wondering how the Babe or Lou Gehrig or any other major leaguer would act if a black player was on their team. Would they insist he stay in the same hotel? Would they refuse to attend a dinner where he wasn't wanted? Would they take the field if another team refused to compete as long as he was on the roster? Would they break a law that denied his rights as a human being? You can't answer these questions, but you do know this: On 23 august 1934, a team of fifteen- and sixteen-year-old kids from Springfield, Massachusetts, wouldn't eat, sleep, or play ball in Gastonia, North Carolina, unless their African-American teammate was treated with the same respect, regard, and dignity as all the other players.

News of what happened in Gastonia reaches Springfield before you do. Reporters from the local papers drive to Hartford, Connecticut, where they board the train to get the first scoops. They all hear the same story: a team is a team is a team.

A huge crowd greets you when the train pulls into Union Station. Signs calling you "HEROES" and "CHAMPS" bob up and down over the people's heads. Flashbulbs light up the sky like fireworks. Even Mayor Martens is there to get a photo of himself shaking hands with Bunny while his parents look on. You can see in their proud eyes what their son has learned in his heart: he is more than a rabbit. He is more than an all-star baseball player. He is a human being with friends who've hit a home run for human beings everywhere.

EPILOGUE

ERNEST "BUNNY" TALIAFERRO lettered in football, basketball, and baseball in each of his four years at Springfield Technical High School in Massachusetts. He was also each team's captain. In 1934 and 1935 he led the football team to city championships and was named All-City. As a pitcher for the baseball team, he amassed nineteen wins without a single loss. Several colleges offered him athletic scholarships, but he turned them down when his father insisted the schools compensate him for having taught his son all he knew about sports. Bunny stayed in Springfield, married elevator operator Julia "Sweets" Addison, and helped raise six children. Never missing a day of work in twenty years at Fisk Tire and playing basketball and baseball in the Springfield Industrial League, he put every one of them through college without once mentioning his athletic accomplishments or the events that took place in Gastonia, North Carolina.

Bunny died on his fiftieth birthday in 1967.

JOHNNY COFFEY worked and played baseball in the Springfield Industrial League for the Gilbert and Barker Manufacturing Company. He married Rita Sheridan, with whom he had three children, and served for fourteen years in the Massachusetts State Legislature where he was a persistent and outspoken advocate of human rights.

DANNY KEYES graduated from Boston College Law School. At the age of 28, he became the youngest presiding judge in Massachusetts history—a record that still stands. He married Gertrude Dewire and together they raised six children. An usher at Bunny Taliaferro's funeral, he told the *Springfield Republican* that the Post 21 team's decision to withdraw from the tournament in Gastonia "wasn't just the right thing to do; it was the only thing to do."

TONY KING worked and played basketball and baseball for the American Bosch Manufacturing Company in the Springfield Industrial League. During World War II, he served with the United States Navy as part of a ground crew in England that inspected planes being prepared for the Allied invasion of Europe: D-Day. After the war, he met and married co-worker Charlotte Hall. "It would have been easier to suit up and take the field," he says of the Post 21 team's decision to return to Springfield rather than play in the American Legion tournament, "but we refused to desert a guy who'd played with us all season. It didn't matter the color of his skin. He was our teammate. We did what was right."

THE CITY OF SPRINGFIELD erected in 2003 a monument honoring the American Legion Post 21 team at the Forest Park Baseball Field where Bunny and his teammates played. Danny Keyes wrote the statement that appears on the memorial. His retelling of the heroic vote that took place in 1934 concludes: "It was an act of loyalty and love for their friend and brother which sent a message that bigotry has no place in the game of baseball or in the game of life—a message proclaimed by a band of 16-year-old kids a generation before the barrier of racial prejudice of Major League Baseball was torn down with the recruitment of another black, Jackie Robinson."

AMERICAN LEGION POST 21 of Springfield dropped baseball in 1935 to protest the national organization's tolerance of racial discrimination; the American Legion retaliated by removing every mention of the team from its official records. Seventy-six years later, the team was revived. At its opening game on 13 June 2010, Tony King and Danny Keyes, the two surviving members of the historic team, threw out the ceremonial first pitches. Massachusetts Governor Deval Patrick awarded honorary rings to Tony, Danny, and Bunny's daughter, Linda Taliaferro. Tony and Danny were also honored with first pitches on 22 August 2010 before a Boston Red Sox game at Fenway Park. "What those kids said so loudly in 1934 resonates through the decades," Linda told the *Springfield Republican*. "And in one voice!"

SPRINGFIELD COLLEGE honored the 1934 American Legion Post 21 baseball team with the first annual Humanics Achievement Award in 2014. Ninety-six-year-old Tony King, the team's captain and sole surviving member, was the recipient.

ABOUT THE BOOK

The final incarnation of this book would not have been possible without generous contributions from Diane Lyn Andersen (my first and most exacting editor), William Goldman (my writing mentor who told me the book was "brilliant" and not to change a word), Steve Strimer (who published it without changing a word), Dix McComus (whose exquisite painting graces the cover), Tony King and Danny Keyes (who lived the story and shared their memories with me), Linda Taliaferro (who provided important insights for the character based on her father, Bunny Taliaferro), John P. O'Connor (who provided all the research any writer could ever need), Garry Brown (who wrote the most and the best of the research) Barbara Dismuke (who introduced me to the story of the Post 21 team), and Tim Murray (who raised the money to erect the monument to the team that stands in Springfield's Forest Park).

The life of this book after its publication will be due in large part to Superintendent Daniel Warwick (whose vision is to make sure this story is known to every student in every Springfield public school), Mayor Dominic Sarno (who continues to conduct read alouds for more Springfield students than anyone can count), Director Guy McClain (who will mount at the

Springfield Historical Museum a permanent exhibit honoring the team's heroic action in 1934), and the selfless, indefatigable efforts of Mike Borecki and Brian "the Expediter" Collins.

Thank you all.

Different versions of *We Called Him Bunny* have appeared in *Elysian Quarterly Review, Equinox, Alden Street Review, the new renaissance,* and the illustrated children's book *A Home Run for Bunny.*

ABOUT THE AUTHOR

Richard Andersen has written twenty-nine books, including novels, critical studies, books on writing, a biography, a children's book, and an examination of contemporary education: *Arranging Deck Chairs on the Titanic.*

A former Fulbright Professor, Karolyi Foundation Fellow, and James Thurber Writer in Residence at Ohio State University, Richard teaches writing and literature at Springfield College, where he was honored with the college's Excellence in Teaching Award and nominated for the Carnegie Foundation's United States Professor of the Year Award.

A sports enthusiast, Richard was a bronze-medal winner in the 1976 New York City Bicentennial Marathon and was a member of the 2004 silver-medal winning basketball team from Massachusetts in the New England Senior Olympics.

Richard and his wife Diane Lyn live in Montague, Massachusetts.